Itchybald Scratchet

Return from Rainbow Ravine

by

Sue C. Medcalf

Published

by

Sable Publishing House

PO Box 107, Wellington TA21 1BD, Somerset,
UNITED KINGDOM

ISBN 978 1 906255 65 7

9 781906 255657

Itchybald Scratchet

Return from Rainbow Ravine

Published by Sable Publishing House, July 2014
Cover design © Sable Publishing House
Illustrations: Nicole Poulsom – **colepoul@gmail.com**

*   *   *   *   *   *   *

About the Author

Sue C. Medcalf

 Born in Bedford (UK), the eldest of four, Sue left school with average exam results. Ever since, her passion has been her family, and she now has two adult sons and eight wonderful grandchildren. Until now, her family and work have been too demanding to commit to writing a book.

Having finally put pen to paper, finding the experience rewarding and therapeutic, Sue is now involved in an ongoing writing project, capitalising on her interest and research into badgers and wildlife in general, along with their behaviour and habitat. Her intention is to encourage children of all ages to benefit, enjoy and learn from reading.

Her family moved from Bedford to Somerset in the nineteen nineties, thereby enriching her understanding and enjoyment of nature and the countryside. The inevitable conflict between the need for human development owing to the increase in population and wildlife has been motivational to her writing.

* * * * * * *

About the Illustrator

Nicole Poulsom

Born and raised in Durban, South Africa, the eldest of two, Nicole was raised in an animal-friendly home and always had some form of pet. They were usually cats or a dog but have also included rats, mice, fish and the odd budgie. She even helped catch snakes for her younger brother's collection. Nicole loved drawing and painting from a young age, but lacked the confidence to use her talent until now.

Now living in the UK, Nicole is happily settled in Kent with her husband, cat and spaniel, who all came over from South Africa. Having developed a passion with British wildlife, she is delighted to be included in this amazing project about Itchybald Scratchet and his friends.

"It is a wonderful thought that people reading this series will enjoy the characters created by the author. I hope my interpretation of Itchy and his friends enhances the story and enjoyment when reading about their adventures."

* * * * * * *

DEDICATION

This publication is dedicated to my dear mother, Mavis Yvonne Martin (1935–2014), and also my family, who mean so much to me and whose love, support and encouragement made it possible.

The inspiration for writing is from my sister, Dawn, without whom the *Itchybald Scratchet* series wouldn't have started. Dawn had badgers in her back garden and didn't know what to do about them. I did some research on badgers and their way of life, which lead me to write the book. My sister and I share a similar humour and our badger conversations developed into an amusing story, resulting in this publication.

I would particularly like to thank Nicole for producing all the sketches used in the story and Sable Publishing House for guidance and support through to production. I am also most grateful to John Troughear for applying his considerable knowledge and experience to editing the final version ready for publication. Thanks also to Claire Pickering or Richmond Pickering Ltd for all her valuable help and advice in helping the project come to fruition.

Special thanks go to Pauline Kidner of the Secret World Wildlife Rescue Centre in Highbridge, Somerset for allowing us to use some of their badger pictures in book one. They do a great job caring for wild animals in need. You can learn more by visiting their website www.secretworld.org.

None of this would have been possible without the help and support of my husband, Ian, my family, friends and neighbours, to whom I am indebted.

*　　*　　*　　*　　*　　*　　*

iii

What Happened in Book One?
Itchybald Scratchet – The Tales Begin

Discover the delights of hot worm stew as you join badger Itchybald Scratchet (Itchy) and his friends in an amazing adventure to save Badger Wood. Lured out by the smell of windfall apples and with their sett under threat of upples development, all they need to do is find something to mark the site historical interest so it can't be built on. But will they survive the worsening elements?

Frightened of the cull that meant certain death, would the depths of a disused well spell the end for Itchy? Trapped and alone, would 'Enor Mouse' rescue Itchy from the cold, dark depths before he freezes to death?

Following Great-Auntie Twiddle's disappearance several years ago during a particularly harsh winter, the thought of venturing far from their sett seems a daunting prospect. But they must continue their journey or homes will be destroyed and Badger Wood will be gone forever. No more foraging for berries or acorns, no more night-time trips, they will be forced to find a new sett. With not a moment to lose and destination unknown, no one knew how long it would take ...

The raging river their enemy, the small raft rocks perilously on the waters as they cling on tightly. But with their eyes shut tight, none of them see the geese warning of danger ahead. Can they bring Matty to the surface so she can groom her famous coat? Or will it turn out to be a wild goose chase?

Partial to a slice of cheese and tomato pizza, Norm's eating habits soon land him in trouble ... although his legendary tail gives them the ride of their lives.

Can they really save Badger Wood from the Upples?

Does Rainbow Ravine hold the secret?

Can they reach the end of the rainbow before it vanishes?

Does the sound of upples voices herald danger?

And with the pot of gold stuck fast, how will they ever get out?

Characters in Book Two

Upples – People

Badgers
Itchybald Scratchet
Matty Scratchet
Fidget
Hurryup
3 cubs – Squiggle,
Wriggle and Silky

Mouse
Enor Mouse – Norm

Birds
Aubrey – Owl
Walter – Wood Pigeon
Peter Pheasant –
Postman
Blackbirds

Rabbit

Deer
Daphne

Moles
Guacamoley – Moley
Taco (Moley's brother)

Horse
Shire horse – Neighomi

Geese
Gordon
Graham
Gary
Gerald
Godfrey
Gabriel

Itchybald Scratchet – Return From Rainbow Ravine

Book TWO of his amazing adventures

Itchy could hear upples approaching the muddy ravine they were in and he was sure they would have weapons ready for the impending cull.

"Shhh," he whispered to his friends, putting a claw to his lips. "I think I can hear upples voices on the wind."

Itchy, Matty and Norm stood really still, listening for any sounds from above, their hearts pounding so loud that Itchy was worried the upples might hear them. With the wind howling around them it was hard to hear what they were saying. Matty's fur stood on end, blown about by the wind. Itchy was right, there was the definite sound of upples conversations and a loud cough carried towards them on the wind.

"I'm sure I saw badgers near here," panted the first man, bending over trying to catch his breath.

"I thought so, too," puffed a second voice. "But they're not here now and besides, the drop into the ravine is so steep that they wouldn't have survived the fall."

"We only just missed them!" Gasped the first man again, still bent with his hands on his knees. "We were so close ..."

The three friends held their breath while listening to the upples discussing what to do next.

The ravine had a lip at the top, so Itchy, Matty and Norm pressed themselves into the side as best they could, in an attempt to avoid being seen. Long, thick tufts of grass concealed them from view. Norm, the overlarge mouse, tucked his long tail under and held himself in as best he could. His tummy stuck out even when he turned side on and, with the effort of holding it in, it growled in protest. Norm was hungry.

"What was that?" hissed one of the upples.

"What was what?" said the other, irritated at being held up. "I didn't hear anything. Come on; let's get a move on. It's starting to rain, it's windy and I've spent more than enough time searching for badgers in the mud and cold for one day!"

The three friends hiding in the Ravine

The upples leaned forward as far as they could over the edge in a last-ditch attempt at finding something. Unable to see anything and wary that they might fall, they turned their backs and walked away. Itchy gave a huge sigh of relief and looked at Norm, a mischievous glint sparkling in his dark eyes.

"Whew! That was close," he gasped. "I think we had better find something to eat before your noisy stomach gives us away!"

Itchy looked around him for the first time, scratching his side while observing his surroundings. The bright rainbow had long-since disappeared.

A stream ran through the ravine, which was rocky on the sides, quite muddy underfoot and only a few upples' height in width. Dark green ivy tangled around the tree trunks and weeds grew prolifically. Where the upples had trampled on the ferns and moss, it resembled a damp, muddy brown mess. Rubbish had been left scattered carelessly; a single upples trainer that had seen better days, a drinks can and a plastic bag were nearby.

"There doesn't appear to be much food. Not a pizza in sight," expressed Norm disappointedly. Pizza was his favourite meal and how he longed for a cheese-and-tomato one.

"What are we going to do?" asked Matty raising her tatty eyebrow, with concern in her voice.

Itchy observed her fondly. It would take quite a bit of grooming to sort out her coat, if only they had the time.

"At least there are plenty of worms and acorns." Itchy and Matty scratched at a nearby tree to demonstrate his point. "I know Norm might not be so keen, but he will have to make do until we can find a bin for him to rummage in." Itchy laughed, remembering the mess Norm had got into in the upples garden a few nights ago when he had gone in head-first.

The look on Norm's face said it all. He was sick of worms, but he didn't seem to have much choice in the matter. The thought of proper pizza made his stomach rumble even more.

"Look," said Itchy, smiling kindly, trying to be sensible. "We will just have to make the best of it until we decide what to do. Badger Wood is our main concern. We need to move this gold and get out of here before anyone returns. Does anyone have any suggestions?"

The three friends looked at one another, unsure what to do next. The night air was becoming colder and a frost was in the air. The ground was already hardening and slowly turning crispy white. Hunger getting the better of them, they decided to eat worms first and then investigate the other end of the ravine, to see if they could find something with which to move the treasure.

Using their claws to cover the shiny golden pot with weeds and dirt, Itchy and Matty did their best to disguise it. Norm also helped by using his long tail to gather up leaves. The trio then pushed it under a gorse bush before finding an escape route.

Itchy, Matty and Norm cover the pot with debris

Rummaging around in the hardening mud, stopping to nibble on worms in the moonlight every so often, they were so preoccupied that they didn't see a small mound of earth erupting through the long muddy grass close by.

Behind them a small black mole appeared with a beautiful velvety face. It had beady, shiny black eyes and its whiskers moved wildly from side to side as its pink nose sniffed at the night air.

"Who is it? My sight might not be so good, but I can smell somebody!"

The accent was difficult to understand. What's a foreign mole doing in Rainbow Ravine? wondered Itchy.

"Itchy," replied Itchy. "I'm a badger and my name is Itchybald Scratchet. And who are you?"

"My name is Guacamoley; Moley for short. I came here from Mexico on holiday with my brother, Taco."

With that another mound appeared beside him. Then they heard a slight popping sound and another mole came into view. He looked identical to the first one.

"Meet Taco," Moley said, smiling proudly.

Moley and Taco meet the three friends

I sometimes eat moles, thought Itchy to himself, but I don't know that I would like foreign ones.

The three friends exchanged glances at one another in amazement. They hadn't expected to find anyone down there, let alone a foreign mole and his brother. After discussing their dilemma amongst themselves, they decided to confide in the moles to see if they would help move the treasure; although being so small, Itchy doubted that they would be much help at all.

Moley said, "We know of some other badgers who live nearby. With their help, I'm sure we could find a way out of the ravine up to the top. Once on the other side there is a cobbled lane that wiggles and wiggles round. It's sheltered by bushes but you would be on your way back to Badger Wood by the time anyone saw you."

Somewhat relieved, Itchy looked at Moley.

"Do you think they would be willing to help?" he asked, concern in his voice.

"Their sett is further down in the ravine. They will surely have heard of Badger Wood and will want to help you save your friends.

Badgers are very social animals and I'm sure they won't be averse to helping you move the gold under such circumstances."

With that, the two moles disappeared underground again, leaving a mound of mud in their wake as they quickly snaked their way down the ravine.

Itchy, Matty and Norm ran after the mole tracks as fast as they could, stumbling and tripping through the mud. Eventually, they came to a small doorway almost hidden from view. It was on the far side of the ravine and was covered in leaves. After moving them to one side, the moles knocked hard on the wooden door.

"Who is it?" a deep badger's voice from inside called out. He sounded slightly annoyed. "Don't you know what time it is? It's nearly dawn and I was just nodding off to sleep!"

A sleepy badger opens his door

"It's me!" Moley said urgently. "I have some friends here in urgent need of help."

A sleepy badger slowly opened the door a crack, blinking and shielding his eyes from the early morning light. Blackbirds, their dark, feathered wings spread open like upple fingers, flew low overhead.

"Well come in, then," said the badger with a sigh of resignation, knowing he wouldn't get any peace now and not wishing to appear rude in front of his visitors. If it was as urgent as the mole had inferred then it would have been bad-mannered not to help.

The moles entered the sett first, followed by the others. The front room was comfortable but sparsely furnished. A large, squashy brown armchair dominated the room and was surrounded by cushions scattered on the floor. A fire glowed softly in the grate with a worn patchwork mat in front of it. It was not as homely or cosy as Itchy and Matty's home.

"Sorry to wake you," said Itchy, scratching his side, "but we need some help. I don't know if you have heard, but Badger Wood is about to be destroyed. The upples intend to build on our home and surrounding fields as they develop the area for upples habitation."

"Well we can't have that," replied the badger, yawning and smoothing his fur down with a paw over his sleepy head. "How can we be of assistance?"

"We need some help to move a pot of gold that we have found at the end of the rainbow. The pot is stuck fast and is said to refill whenever there is a rainbow. If we can put enough of the gold in the ground at Badger Wood, the upples may declare it a historical site and think twice about building on it."

"And!" gasped Matty, her fur more on end than ever in her excitement, "if we all help we can remove the gold and get back faster."

"First things first," said the tired badger, rubbing his eyes. "Introductions. My name is Fidget. I have lived in this sett for several years now with my family."

Equally sleepy badgers of all sizes, five in all, including Fidget, emerged. The front room was quite crowded with the three friends and the moles as well.

"This is my family," Fidget announced, standing upright and puffing out his chest proudly. "This is my wife, Hurryup, and our three cubs Squiggle, Wriggle and Silky."

To their surprise, Silky was pure white, almost sparkling. She was an albino badger with pink eyes.

"Albinos are white with no colouration to their fur owing to a genetic difference in their make-up," volunteered Hurryup, sensing their surprise and pleased to be showing off her family.

She went on to explain how Silky must take after a few other badger relatives born years ago, with the same abnormally white coat and beautiful pink eyes.

Silky smiled shyly, aware of how unusual she was. Her fur was soft, silky and downy.

Matty thought she was the most beautiful badger cub she had ever seen. Silky cuddled up to the other cubs for warmth. None of them seemed impressed at being woken. Badger Wood seemed a long way off and therefore, in their eyes, was nothing to do with them. They would rather be snuggled up together all warm and comfortable.

"Have you eaten?" asked Fidget, now wide-awake and anxious to see to his guests.

"Thank you, but we've had some worms and acorns. Well, all except Norm, that is. He's our big mouse friend here. He prefers pizza but there isn't any round here; I expect he's starving by now."

"We have a few apples and some dry bread, if that will do?"

Fidget hurried off to find them, while Hurryup pulled up other chairs and cushions for them all to make themselves comfortable.

Norm was delighted! He didn't mind apples and although they were small, they were quite sweet and made a change to worms. He tucked in to his dinner hungrily and then wiped his paws and whiskers clean not long after.

The older badgers sat long into the day, hatching a plan to help save Badger Wood, while the cubs went back to bed.

Moley and Taco left them all to it. They waved the badgers goodbye and returned to their home, preferring to be in their tunnel. Meanwhile the badgers and Norm settled down to sleep. Nothing could be done until night-time, anyway, by which time hopefully the upples would have given up long ago and gone home.

The following evening Itchy, Matty, Norm and their new friends started to look for something to put the gold in. Whatever they used needed to be strong enough to survive the journey back to Badger Wood.

"Maybe we could use takeaway containers or carrier bags. Perhaps they would be strong enough," suggested Fidget as the badgers searched long and hard through the tangled undergrowth and the rubbish left behind by the upples.

"One problem we've overlooked, though," said Itchy as the bags and takeaway boxes started to topple out of his arms. "Has anyone thought about how we're going to carry them once they're filled with gold. Surely they will be too heavy for us."

Itchy, Matty and Norm search the ravine

"I have an idea," Matty declared, scratching her matted coat while looking at Fidget. "Have you seen anything on your travels with wheels? We could do with using something that we could pull along."

"You wouldn't believe the things upples throw into this beautiful ravine," said Fidget, shaking his head sadly.

Fidget was fed up trying to clear the rubbish from his surroundings. Hearing tales about the stunning features of Badger Wood had made him sad at the untidy state of the ravine they called home. The upples wouldn't like it if the badgers made such a mess or left rubbish lying around their neighbourhood. Left to their own devices they would ruin this beautiful ravine. But occasionally nice upples came and tidied it up, Fidget thought, consoling himself.

"They should take their rubbish home with them. It's a good job we badgers are tidy, clean animals," he said gloomily. "Still, maybe they've left something useful like an old cart or an upples bike," he added with renewed enthusiasm.

The night sky was turning ever colder and the now hard, crisp and white frost shone in the moonlight. The badgers and Norm began exploring, searching for something they could use to pull the gold along.

First they found a wheel from an old upple pushchair, but it was too big and a funny shape. Then they found just one wheel from an upples bicycle, but that was no good, either.

Then Fidget called out: "I think I have found something ... come and look at this!"

Fidget had found just what they were looking for: an old skateboard that had been tossed aside into the undergrowth.

The worn skateboard was painted roughly in red-and-blue stripes. It seemed to be in reasonable condition with the exception of one end, which was jagged and damaged. Some of the wheels wobbled a little when they tried to wheel it along but it was the closest thing they had found to something near suitable.

Fidget finding the skateboard

"Never mind. It's better than nothing. It should take quite a lot of gold and we can all help to move it," smiled Matty, her beautiful dark eyes sparkling.

Itchy, Matty and their friends loaded the gold into the bags and takeaway cartons they had collected, ready to put them onto the skateboard. The only problem now was how to move it without the upples seeing them.

"Fidget, do you think we could all help dig another tunnel to the top of the ravine?" asked Itchy, now keen to find a way out.

"Of course," said Fidget. "We badgers are all excellent diggers. If we start right away we will have it done in no time. Then we can move the gold underground so it will remain unseen."

"If he doesn't mind, we can use Norm's tail and wrap around the broken end. That way he can pull the skateboard through the tunnel and the rest of us can help push from behind."

"Certainly," replied Norm, keen to help his badger friends.

The badgers helped to get the skateboard ready and then Itchy, Matty and Fidget set to work digging. Up and up they went at a steady pace to the top of the ravine. It took several nights for the badgers to move such an amount of soil and luckily, it wasn't frozen solid. They kept reminding themselves why they were doing it, which kept them going. The badgers were exhausted and filthy by the time they had finished.

The following evening they were just preparing to start taking the gold up to the surface, when they heard a thud outside the sett.

"What's that?" said Matty, her fur once more sticking up in clumps, despite her best efforts to remain well groomed.

"You lot stay quiet while I go and see," answered Fidget.

As he pulled the door open to their sett, he could see a pheasant with beautiful brown-and-blue plumage. He was huffing and puffing, complaining to himself while straightening his feathers in annoyance. Fidget could see he was cross.

"It's Peter!" Itchy exclaimed, looking over Fidget's shoulder. "What are you doing here? For a postman you are a long way from Badger Wood and I know you don't normally fly far."

Peter pheasant outside the sett

"I've been looking for you everywhere! I came to tell you something ..." gasped the pheasant, grumpy and exhausted from his flight. "The upples are conducting a study on the land in Badger Wood for their new houses! We are at a loss as to what to do ... Daphne is thinking of taking her fawns and leaving! All the woodland animals are in hiding, afraid to leave their homes."

"Slow down and catch your breath a moment! We've found just what we need to declare the area a historic site!" volunteered Matty. "We are ready to move it and we will be back as soon as we can. Please tell the other animals not to worry; we are on our way home."

After a short rest, Peter flew back to the Wood to inform their friends of the good news.

By now the ravine animals had heard about Badger Wood and how Itchy and his friends were trying to save it. Everyone was talking about Itchy, Matty and Norm's brave journey to try and save the area from upples habitation.

As soon as darkness fell, Norm climbed into the tunnel and the badgers pushed the skateboard inside after him.

"I don't like being in the dark much," Norm complained, closing his eyes against the loose bits of soil. He brushed the damp mud from his fur. "Let's get this skateboard out into the open as quick as we can."

With Norm's strong, very long tail twisted round the broken end of the skateboard, he began to climb up the tunnel. Straining hard, he pulled the gold along on the skateboard behind him. Itchy, Matty and Fidget took it in turns to push uphill, until they slowly reached top of the ravine and emerged into the fresh air.

"Thank goodness!" exclaimed Norm, wiping the dirt from his paws while undoing his tail. He was relieved to be out of the dark tunnel.

After making sure the gold was safe and checking that they hadn't dropped any in their haste, they all sat on the grass resting in the moonlight.

"We can't rest long," said Itchy. "Our friends are relying on us."

The badgers and Norm resting

Itchy, Matty and Norm waved goodbye to Fidget and his family and set off down the wiggly lane, wheeling the skateboard along behind them. It seemed to go better on the road surface but it was quite noisy. If they tried to wheel it on the verge it was too bumpy and the wheels got clogged up with partly frozen dirt. At least at this time of night there were no upples about. Also, there were plenty of thick gorse bushes by the side of the lane to shelter under.

The three friends had walked for an hour or so, when they heard someone calling them from behind.

"Wait for us! Wait for us!" the voice called out.

It was Fidget with Hurryup and her cubs trailing behind, their little paws running as fast as they could to keep up with their father.

"After you left, Hurryup and I discussed the state of the ravine and all the rubbish the upples leave behind. Anyway ..." He paused, puffing and panting from the exertion. "Anyway, we thought that if it's okay with you, we would make our home in Badger Wood with you guys."

"That would be lovely!" Matty exclaimed. She looked at Itchy and Norm for approval. Matty had really taken to the cubs and Silky was just adorable.

"Of course!" replied Itchy and Norm in unison and they all laughed.

"Well that's settled, then. But there is still no guarantee the upples won't build on it. We may all be out of a home yet," said Itchy.

"Then we will cross that bridge together," replied Fidget confidently. "The ravine is not what it was, so this will be a new beginning for us."

Their progress was slow now they had the cubs in tow. Their little paws were tired as they weren't used to walking on a road surface. But while the journey would take a bit longer, Itchy and Matty couldn't bring themselves to leave them behind. And Norm was still very grateful to the badgers for finding him apples when he had been hungry, so he was in agreement, too.

As they rounded a corner of the wiggly road, in the distance they could see some farm buildings in the grey morning light. A large stone farmhouse was partially shrouded in the mist and remnants of a puff of smoke came from the chimney. A dim light shone through a chink in one of the curtains but the rest were closed fully. Hopefully, the upples were still asleep.

The farmhouse sat at the end of a rough muddy track. An upples Land Rover was parked outside along with a tractor, its huge wheels caked in mud. A cowshed stood nearby with a few chickens pecking at the ground.

It started to drizzle on the already damp and muddy friends. There was no hope for Matty's coat, which was a mess once more. Itchy's foot was hurting and he was still limping from his fall into the well, when he had been rescued by Norm's legendary tail.

Even though it had happened some time ago, his foot almost always ached now, especially in these damp conditions or when he walked too far.

The farmhouse in the early morning light

Then Norm's stomach started rumbling again – he was hungry, as usual. Together they decided they would seek shelter and see if they could find any food.

Heavy rain clouds hid the winter sun, but they could just make out an old barn to the right of them near the lane. Wooden sides and a corrugated iron roof made up the structure. The back of the barn faced the road, so no danger of being seen. Inside it was filled to the roof with straw and pale golden hay bales piled high. Some had spilled onto the old, uneven floor, to be used as food and shelter for the farm animals over the coming winter months.

They would use the barn to shield them from view during daylight. After all, it would be a shame to be caught by the upples now, just as they were on their way home. Too risky to travel by the lane for a few hours, they might as well rest.

The rain was now heavy and they cautiously entered the barn, in case any upples were up and about, starting work early. The noise from the wobbly wheels on the skateboard would be more difficult to hide, though. Itchy, Matty, Norm and the other badgers crept towards the straw. It looked warm and inviting.

Now closer, they could see in the dim light an old shire horse standing in the corner. She was the biggest horse the friends had ever seen. She had a beautiful chestnut brown coat, with a white stripe down her nose and very big hooves. She shifted in surprise and whinnied when she caught sight of Itchy. On her back was a thick dark green horse blanket to keep out the cold. Her upple owner must be kind and caring, Itchy decided.

"Hello," said the horse. Her large brown eyes twinkled as she chewed. "It's nice to have some visitors. It gets awfully lonely in here. Who are you?" she asked, surveying the newcomers.

"My name is Itchybald Scratchet; Itchy to my friends. This is my wife, Matty, and our friends Norm and Fidget. He and his family are coming to live near us. We are all on a journey to help save our friends and Badger Wood."

"What's your name?" enquired Matty, wide-eyed; she was struck by the sheer size of the beast. She had never seen such a large animal. Little did she know that hundreds of years ago shire horses were ridden by knights in shining armour. Big and strong, they were ideally suited to carry heavy upples. Nowadays, they were more used to ploughing fields occasionally or pulling a cart.

"My name is Neighomi," the shire horse replied. "And I think what you are doing to save your friends is wonderful! My upple owners are kind and caring so I can't complain. Not at all like those who only think of themselves and not us animals. They provide me with a warm shelter and plenty of food. If it's cold they put a blanket on me. In return I help them by pulling cartloads of straw or ploughing fields. Can I help you in any way?"

Neighomi

"We just need to rest awhile," said Matty, tired but content to have somewhere to rest.

Norm's stomach rumbled once more and they all smiled at one another.

"Sorry, I could do with some pizza, really," sighed Norm apologetically. "Do you know where I could get any from? I'm awfully famished."

"The upples bake their own food here and tend to eat it all. They don't like waste, you see. But you could always have a look around. I think there might be some acorns under the oak tree," replied Neighomi.

Norm sighed and looked down at the barn floor, feeling very fed up. Nothing very appetising here either, he thought glumly. I guess acorns will have to do, then. Ever since Norm had got trapped in a pizza factory years ago, he had loved pizza, and if ever he could do with some, it was now.

The friends all snuggled down into the straw to get a few hours' sleep. There was still a long way to go to save Badger Wood.

Just as a hazy moon was rising, the rain having stopped, Itchy woke up. Matty was still asleep, along with the rest of the badgers. They were all huddled together, but Norm was nowhere to be seen.

"Have you seen Norm?" Itchy asked Neighomi.

"No," replied the horse, stretching her neck and yawning, "I've been asleep myself."

"Then where is he?" asked Matty, now wide-awake, concern growing. Her tatty coat was sticking up all over the place and covered in straw.

They roused the others but none of them knew what to do or where to look first.

"He can't be far away," declared Fidget as he and Hurryup went outside.

"Maybe he's just gone for a walk," volunteered Neighomi kindly.

"If he's not careful the upples will find him," responded Itchy. "Surely you must know they don't like badgers and it's culling season."

"We'll all help look for him," said Neighomi reassuringly, her dark eyes kind. "He's probably gone off in search of acorns ... or pizza."

Itchy and Matty went outside into the damp, early evening air. They called and called while

Neighomi looked in the distance. Being taller she hoped she could see farther away and perhaps spot Norm. Then she could call him with her loud neigh. Norm is so big you couldn't exactly miss him.

The friends search for Norm

They searched all around the farmyard as close to the house and the cowshed as they dare, but there was still no sign of Norm.

"Norm! Nooorm, where are you?" called Itchy loudly in his deep badgers voice.

"There's nothing for it. We'll have to leave him behind. The others are waiting and we need to save Badger Wood. We'll come back and find him afterwards. Don't worry," Fidget said, patting Matty fondly, 'he'll be quite safe."

Then Neighomi had an idea.

"I can help you get back to Badger Wood quicker," she said. "My upple owners and I are due to take a small cart of straw to another farm near Badger Wood, if you could wait a bit longer. After all, I can take you quite a way with all that gold. You can all hide in the back."

As they now didn't have Norm to help them, it seemed the only choice they had left. It was a good job Fidget and Hurryup were with them, for the gold was too heavy to manage alone. At least if they could get it back to Badger Wood, the other animals could help.

Matty found an old sack in the corner of the barn, so they put the gold into that. It was easier to manage than the skateboard and it would sit nicely under the straw with them.

In the early morning light, Itchy and Matty climbed into the cart while Fidget and Hurryup handed the cubs to them. It was with heavy hearts that they loaded the gold, for none of them really wanted to leave without Norm.

Climbing onto Neighomi's cart

Only the sound of the birds singing their dawn chorus and Matty's silent sniffing could be heard above the clip-clop, clip-clop of Neighomi's hooves, which echoed down the lane. They all missed Norm already.

Plodding along in the darkness and upset at Norm's disappearance, none of them noticed a hole in the corner of the sack containing the gold until they heard the tinkling of coins falling.

"What's that noise?" whispered Itchy.

"Oh no! No!" cried Matty. "Look, Itchy, some of the gold has fallen out of a hole in the sack!"

"Quick! Stop the cart!" Itchy hissed to Neighomi.

Neighomi pretended she had a stone in her shoe, so the upple was distracted with her hooves. Scraping one hoof from side to side on the stony ground, she said: "I will keep the upple busy while you all pick it up. Don't worry. He won't suspect a thing."

Itchy, Matty and the badgers set about picking up as much of the gold as they could find. It wasn't long before they heard geese flying overhead, the distinctive sound of their calls echoing on the early morning sky. They were making a lot of noise as there was an upple about. The next moment they swooped down onto the lane, as they landed one by one in formation.

Geese landing in the lane

"Hello," said Gordon. "You look as though you could do with some help here."

Itchy burst out laughing. "My, my! What are *you* doing here, Gordon?" he exclaimed. "We haven't seen you and your friends since you rescued us from the river. And look! You have all your lifeguard friends with you."

"We were just on a practice flight when I looked down and saw you and Matty in the lane. Are you all right? I see you have made some new friends."

Itchy introduced Fidget and his family to the lifeguard geese.

"We are so pleased to see you all!" said Itchy.

"You can say that again. Would you mind helping us retrieve the gold?" Matty asked. "Norm has gone missing so we need all the help we can get."

With one eye on the upple who was busy with Neighomi's hooves, Gordon replied, "Certainly and then we will look for Norm. We're more likely to spot him from overhead." He could see how worried Itchy and Matty were and was keen to help.

Gordon the goose, along with Gary, Gabriel and the others, collected as much gold in their beaks as they could, tucking it into their feathers. They were only too aware that it needed to be buried in the ground at Badger Wood as soon as possible if they were going to stop the upples building on it.

At last Neighomi couldn't keep the upple occupied any longer. There didn't appear to be a stone in her hoof and neither could the upple figure out why his horse was reluctant to move. She was normally so easy-going and placid. He put it down to all the noise the geese were making, upsetting her.

"Come on, old girl," said the upple, patting Neighomi affectionately. "Not far now."

"Quick!" whispered Gordon urgently to Itchy. "You had better climb onto the cart with the remainder of the gold before you are seen. We will hide the rest under the bushes until the coast is clear. When it is safe, I will see to it that the other geese carry it to Badger Wood and we will sprinkle some of it over the field."

"Thank you," replied Itchy gratefully. This was the second time the geese had come to their rescue. "But what about Norm? He's still missing."

"Don't worry," replied Gordon. "Leave it to us and we will have a look for him. He's probably curled up fast asleep somewhere having eaten loads of acorns."

The geese took to the cloudy grey sky, carrying the gold as best they could.

Safely back on the cart, the badgers huddled together in the straw, holding the sack close. As it slowly moved away down the lane the slow, soft clip-clop of Neighomi's hooves soon lulled them off to sleep.

They were woken by upples voices. Itchy and Matty hardly dared to move. They had arrived at the farm near Badger Wood. The upple who had driven the cart brought it to a stop, readjusted his woolly hat over his ears then jumped down having been invited into the farmhouse for a cup of tea.

With dawn now breaking and a mist lying pale and low across the open fields, the badgers climbed down clutching their sack of gold coins.

"Badger Wood can't be far now," declared Itchy, relieved to be home nearly.

As Badger Wood came into view, Itchy and Matty's heart gave a leap – it was always good to come home. The familiar trees and fields beyond looked so beautiful in the morning sky.

Fidget and Hurryup were delighted at the prospect of setting up a new sett in such lovely surroundings. What's more, they now had new neighbours.

It didn't take long for the woodland creatures to realise that Itchy, Matty and some new friends had arrived back home. As they entered the clearing all the animals were there to welcome them home. Peter Pheasant had told them all that Itchy had found the gold, but some had hardly dared to believe it.

The sound of the animals cheering overwhelmed Matty. Not only had they found the gold, but they had also made new friends. The only thing making them sad now was the fact that they didn't have Norm with them.

"We have the gold!" announced Itchy triumphantly, standing on an old tree stump. "But," he said cautiously, "we must get it in the ground as soon as we can. The upples have already been to survey the far field. The geese have kindly helped us by sprinkling some of it onto the soil in the next field, but we are running out of time!"

Noisily, the animals began arguing amongst themselves about the best way to distribute the remaining treasure. Aubrey the owl, being wise, thought he knew the best way, but Peter Pheasant disagreed. Walter the wood pigeon waved his wings angrily at them both to stop them arguing. The rabbit, however, couldn't see what all the fuss was about – they had the gold, didn't they? And Daphne and her fawns were convinced they would be safe, seeing all the arguing as a complete waste of time.

Itchy stands on an old tree stump

"Stop! Stop!" Itchy shouted. "We must work together! We are all working towards the same cause. We are, after all, trying to prevent the upples from building on our land near our homes. It's no good arguing amongst ourselves. We all want what's best for everyone!"

All the animals fell silent as they thought about Itchy's words. He was right. They were better off working together.

It was really cold that night as they set about the task ahead. Itchy, Matty, Fidget and Hurryup, along with their cubs and the other woodland animals, all started to spread the treasure around. The cubs helped by digging small holes to put it in, but the ground was too hard.

Fidget said, "Don't worry; we can't bury it too deep, anyway. The upples need to see the gold right under their noses or they will miss it."

Fidget had seen more upples than any of the others and knew them well enough to realise that most of them would only give the ground a cursory glance. Upples are not very observant, he decided. But when they had found a small amount, Fidget hoped the upples would get greedy and search for more. Surely if they found enough gold they would leave the fields alone and find another site for their houses ... After all, there must be an area nearer the town that wouldn't affect the wildlife, thought Itchy to himself.

Darkening clouds formed in the winter sky as the weather closed in and it started to snow. Itchy had never seen snow as deep as this. Fresh, fluffy and white, it fell silently. Softly, like cotton wool, it drifted down onto Badger Wood, muffling the sounds of the woodland animals. Soon, it was an upple-width deep.

They woke the next day to a winter wonderland. The wood was transformed and looked beautiful in the pale moonlight with the branches loaded with snow. The cubs were delighted they had never seen snow before and they enjoyed playing in it. Silky almost disappeared it was so deep, but she could hide and leap out to make the other cubs jump, much to her delight.

Badgers playing in the snow

Itchy and Fidget left the sett reluctantly, to rummage around in the hope of finding berries the birds may have missed, or even windfall apples, a particular favourite.

Adult badgers don't like snow very much and stay in their sett as much as they can. But with extra mouths to feed, Itchy knew they would have difficulty finding extra food beneath the snow.

"It would be better not to wander too far," Itchy warned Fidget as he moved further away. "I fell down a disused well once. If it hadn't been for Norm and his huge tail, I don't think I would be here now."

"I wonder where he is?" said Fidget.

They both knew that with this fresh snowfall there was no hope of leaving the others to go in search of him.

The two badgers searched in all the familiar places to try to find extra food. A few soggy apples and some small berries was all they could find, with food in short supply now. They would need to be careful and eke out their supplies, saving the best of the food for the cubs. Hopefully, the bad weather wouldn't last too long.

Itchy had a thought: "The only good thing about the snow is that the upples can't travel easily, either," he said.

None of them had seen any upples for several days now.

Several days turned into a week. Every time the badgers thought the snow would thaw, it would snow again. Heavy grey winter clouds chased each other like giant horses across the night sky. Snowstorms and strong winds set the scene. The badgers stayed huddled together in their sett for warmth, hungry but not daring to go out.

They woke one morning to a cracking sound from the trees nearby. The snow was melting and drops of icy water still clung to the branches. Like jewels glistening, they soon began falling under the heat of the early morning sun, melting into small puddles.

In a few days the snow had gone, leaving behind a soggy brown mess of leaves and mud. But with the thaw came the upples.

Arriving noisily in vans, they wore fluorescent coats and funny yellow hats. The upples shouted to one another across the fields as they paced up and down, pegging out the site and measuring the field in readiness for drawing up their plans. They had notebooks in hand and would stop periodically to write something down. But still they didn't see the gold.

"What can we do?" asked Matty worriedly, scratching her side once more.

Her fur doesn't look too bad lately, thought Itchy, smiling fondly.

"I don't know," Itchy replied eventually, looking equally concerned. "Fidget is right. These upples can't see anything unless it's right under their nose. Some of the gold must have got buried a bit deeper with all this snow that we have had lately. I think we may have to try to bring some up to the surface again."

"Isn't that a bit risky, though?" answered Fidget. "The upples are here most of the time now and we can't risk being seen."

"We could all go out tonight and move it," Matty said, desperate to know her home was safe. "If we all move the gold nearer the surface, with luck the upples might find some tomorrow."

And so it was agreed. Fidget and Hurryup would take it in turns to stay near the cubs while Itchy and Matty dug in the field further away from their sett.

The sky was clear and the moon was shining brightly when they set off. Itchy had noticed a few black boxes strapped to trees around the wood since they had been back. Walter wood pigeon had informed him that the upples had put them there but no one knew why. Perhaps they were a new type of nesting box for the birds. As the badgers passed by, the box gave a clicking sound and Silky, ever curious, looked straight at it. But nothing seemed to happen, so the badgers went on their way.

Silky in Badger Wood

Hours went by with the badgers busy rummaging about in the dirt looking for treasure and muddy worms to eat. Dawn was soon breaking and it was nearly time to return to the sett but Matty, unseen by the others, had wandered to the boundary of the field. Suddenly, they all heard her call out.

"Help! Help!" Matty screamed at the top of her voice.

Itchy rushed to her aid, followed by the other badgers. What on earth could have happened to her for her to be making such a noise?

Poor Matty had been so busy that she hadn't looked where she was going and had got caught in a badger trap set by the upples. A strong cage surrounded Matty.

"Now what are we going to do?" Itchy asked, turning to Fidget. Then to Matty he said, "Try to stay calm, Matty. We will get you out. Don't worry; try not to get too upset." Itchy hated to see Matty trapped.

Matty was cross now and between tears, sobs and screams she clawed at the metal cage in an attempt to free herself. But all she did was tear her claws and make her mouth sore in the process. Poor Matty was trapped fast and there was nothing the other badgers could do to help her. She jumped up and down as best she could in the confined space, she shook the cage and yelled in rage, but it was to no avail.

The other badgers tried pulling at the cage with their teeth, but Matty remained firmly trapped.

The badgers were so engrossed in trying to release Matty that they didn't hear a van pull up the other side of the hedgerow.

"Quick!" said Itchy. "Everyone under the hedge further down. Hide! I think the upples are coming ..."

The badgers hid from view and could only watch in dismay as Matty was loaded into the back of the van sobbing. On the side of the van it said 'Animal Welfare', whatever that meant, thought Itchy worried. He had never been apart from Matty.

The van drove away in the damp morning air and Itchy, Fidget and the others slowly and dejectedly made their way back to the sett.

Exhausted and frightened, they all fell into a fitful sleep during the daytime. All Itchy could dream of was poor Matty, looking so sad and forlorn, stuck in that cage. He felt powerless.

Next day, the badgers could only wander around looking for her, knowing all along that Matty would probably never be seen again. The poor badgers lost all enthusiasm for moving the gold. Nothing seemed to matter without Matty.

Then they had a surprise. Matty had only been gone for two nights when the following evening, just as they were about to leave the sett, they heard the sound of a badger outside. It was Matty!

"Where have you been?" exclaimed Itchy.

The badgers couldn't believe their eyes.

"I was taken to an upples place," replied Matty excitedly. "They stuck something sharp into my coat and I nearly fell asleep. I could just about keep my eyes open. He put a funny thing on my tummy and then I heard one of the upples say I was having cubs!

Matty returns home

" 'Off you go, girl!', the upple said, 'back to your family.' He spoke so kindly to me and then after they had released me near to where I had become trapped, I ran back here as fast as I could."

No one could believe their ears. Not only was Matty back, but the upples had been kind to her. On top of that was the news that Matty would be having cubs in the spring. Itchy and the other badgers were delighted. There would be a new family of Scratchets to help protect the woodland in the future, thought Itchy proudly.

Spring flowers started to appear slowly in Badgers Wood. Snowdrops and daffodils brightened up the damp, dark soil. Crocuses of yellow and purple budded, along with yellow primroses. Branches on the trees started to shoot new leaves and the birds busied themselves looking for nesting material for their chicks.

Some days the weather was bright and dry now – spring was definitely in the air. Even the sun was beginning to have some warmth in it and the woodland animals began to smile again, rummaging around and preparing their homes for their expected families.

Still the upples hadn't found the gold. This worried Itchy and the badgers. They knew upples were not the most observant but since Matty's trip in the van, they hadn't dare wander too far astray. What was clear, though, was that the surrounding fields and Badger Wood had been quieter of late; it was almost as if the upples had given up. There was only the occasional visit, when an upple or two would peer at them in the darkness. For some reason they had started to visit the Wood at night. But no one came near them. The woodland animals didn't know what to think.

"Have you heard anything about the upples building their homes here?" Itchy asked Peter one evening.

Peter knew all the woodland gossip and usually knew what was happening.

"No," said Peter. "It's all gone really quiet; maybe they have changed their minds."

Then early one spring morning a big grey car arrived carrying an upple family. A couple of tall upples climbed out with their children, one of whom was walking and the other of whom was being carried in a strange-looking sling across the father's body.

Itchy was not used to being awake at this hour and was just making his way back to his sett. He hid in nearby bushes to overhear what was being said.

The male upple looked across and smiled at his wife and children. Then with a broad grin spreading across his face, he said: "This is a wonderful place for us to live and it will be really good for our children to grow up in the countryside. Thank goodness I got that promotion! Just think of the views and the valuable work we will be able to do in protecting this area! I can't wait for our house to be built!"

Itchy couldn't believe his ears! Just one upple home to be built on a field near Badger Wood and the area now protected by the upples!

Itchy listening to the upple

I wonder what bought that about? He thought to himself, a big grin spreading across his handsome badgers face. And they never did find the gold ...

A tremendous banging, hammering sound could be heard as some upples were putting up a big wooden sign that read:

PROTECTED AREA
Rare Albino Badger Sett

Silky had been caught on camera, hidden in one of the black boxes that the badgers had thought were for nesting! They had got what they wanted and the building had stopped. Badger Wood was finally safe ... for now.

Coming Soon ...

Itchybald Scratchet – The Missing Friend

Book THREE of his amazing adventures

Itchy, Matty and the other badgers settle in Badger Wood, but Itchy is still worried about his missing friend. What has happened to Norm? Where can he be? Is he lost somewhere? Will he ever return? Is he even still alive?

Itchy simply had to find his best friend, Norm, who had once saved his life. He felt he owed it to him to travel back and find out what had happened to him.

As Matty has just had her cubs, Itchy and Fidget decide to leave their families at home and do the journey alone. They travel back to the farmyard to see what happened to their friend and why he mysteriously disappeared.

Meanwhile, their friend Enormouse is having an adventure of his own, meeting new animals. Unexpectedly, an upple boy protects him.

Itchy's journey is once again fraught with danger and he and Fidget narrowly escape injury when thrown out of a travelling vehicle. They also mistakenly travel farther than intended, becoming lost in an upple town. Again, they are reliant on help from other animals if they are to find the farm again and, hopefully, their friend.

Reunited, the three return home to Badger Wood. With great excitement, a celebration party is thrown in their honour. The friends are hailed as heroes by the woodland animals. However, all is not as it seems, as Itchy has received a mysterious parcel in his absence. Also, an upple has found some of the gold the badgers scattered around from Rainbow Ravine, which could mean their home is no longer protected.

What will Itchy's next adventure be?

Books in the Series:

Book One – The Tales Begin

Book Two – Return from Rainbow Ravine

Coming Soon:

Book Three – The Missing Friend